D1469465

The
Sheep in

Wolf's Clothing

BOB HARTMAN ■ TIM RAGLIN

LION
CHILDREN'S

Once upon a time there lived a family of sheep.

They grazed on grass, crunched on clover, and played on green pastures.

Except for Little Sheep, that is, who was bored with her peaceful life.

"I'm fed up with baaa–dminton," she bleated. "I don't want to go for another sheep dip. And I definitely don't want to knit another woolly hat!

"I want to do something exciting for a change."

And then, just as she said it, a wolf howled in the distance. And the sheep tossed their rackets, leaped into the pool, dropped their knitting needles, and ran for cover.

All but Little Sheep. Who just stood there. **Alone**. And smiled.

"That's what I want," she cried.

"I want to be a wolf!"

Her parents were horrified at first. But they soon got used to the idea.

"It's just a phase," sighed Mama Sheep.

"She'll grow out of it," Papa Sheep agreed.

And they let her have her way.

Mama Sheep knitted her a woolly wolf suit. Papa Sheep paid for howling lessons. Then, with a kiss and a tear, they sent her away to Wolf School on the other side of the hill.

Little Sheep loved it at first.

She learned how to count to three and

huff-and-puff and blow down

straw houses and stick houses.

She even had a go at brick houses,

much to the admiration of her new classmates.

But when lunchtime came, the menu was not to her liking. Not one bit.

"Lamburgers?" she cringed. "Eee-ewe!"

"I know just what you mean," whispered Little Wolf. "I hate them, too. So on Lamburger Day, my mother always makes me a big bowl of Stu. He was a farmer. Been in the freezer for ages. Want some?"

"No, thank you," she gagged.

"I've got a couple of Chips, too," said Little Wolf. "I think they were Stu's cousins. You could have one of them."

Little Sheep sighed. She couldn't keep this up for ever. And Little Wolf seemed like he wanted to be her friend.

"If you must know," she confessed, "I am a vegetarian."

"I knew there was something different about you," he smiled. "So you only eat people who eat vegetables?"

"No," she said. "I only EAT vegetables."

"Wow, that is different!" said Little Wolf. And he never mentioned it again.

Well, not until he asked his parents if he could invite her over for dinner.

"A vegetarian?" grunted his father from behind the paper. "Probably one of those Fancy Schmancy City Wolves."

"Be nice," said Mother Wolf. "I think I've got a head of cabbage here in the freezer. No. Sorry. That's Farmer Stu's head. But I'll come up with something, dear."

"And I'll catch us some real food," Father Wolf added.

Little Wolf asked Little Sheep the very next day.

"My parents would like to have you for dinner tonight," he said.

"Pardon?" She trembled, ever so slightly.

"They're cooking vegetables and everything," he added.

"Oh, I see," she smiled. "Yes. Sure. Thanks."

But when they walked into Little Wolf's cave that evening, things took a sad and sudden turn for the worse. For there, in the hallway, were **Little Sheep's parents**, tied up and gagged and **ready for the oven.**

"Aww, Mother!" cried Little Wolf. "You know I hate lamb!"

"**Stop your whining!**" Father Wolf called back from the kitchen. "Your mother found a recipe. She's gonna stuff them with the vegetables, douse them in barbecue sauce, and then we'll all be happy."

But Little Sheep was not happy. Not at all. And she decided, right then and there, that it was **time to stop being a wolf.**

"I'm really sorry," she whispered to Little Wolf. "I'm not a wolf at all. I'm a lamb. And these are my parents. You've got to help us. Please!"

"Well, you are my friend," he said. "And even if they were covered with barbecue sauce, I still don't think I would like to eat your parents. So, sure, I'll help. In fact, I've got an idea."

And he ran into the kitchen howling, "Olive! Olive! I've just seen
Farmer Stu's wife, Olive, in the woods!"

"Olive?" cried Father Wolf. "We haven't eaten
any Olives in ages. And that's even a kind of vegetable. I think.
C'mon, Mother!"

So the wolves raced out of the house, in search of Olive.

And as soon as they'd gone,
**Little Sheep
untied her parents** and the three of
them ran away to the other side of the hill.

When Mother and Father Wolf returned at last to the cave, Father Wolf was **disappointed** to find that the sheep had escaped. Mother Wolf was **disappointed** that she couldn't try her new recipe. And Little Wolf was **disappointed** that his friend was gone.

"She had to go home and help her parents with something," he explained.

Little Sheep stayed home, of course. And never went back to Wolf School again.

But once a month, when the moon was full, she would slip into her wolf suit and meet Little Wolf in the woods.

And they would **huff** and they would **puff**. And some pig, somewhere, would always be homeless by morning.